Violet and the Mean and Rotten Pirates

Violet and the Mean and Rotten Pirates

Richard Hamilton

illustrated by

Sam Hearn

BLOOMSBURY
CHILDREN'S
BOOKS

Published by Bloomsbury, New York and London.
Distributed to the trade by Holtzbrinck Publishers.

Library of Congress Cataloging-in-Publication Data
Hamilton, Richard.
Violet and the mean and rotten pirates / by Richard Hamilton; illustrations by
Sam Hearn.
p. cm.
Summary: A group of unusual pirates, whose captain cannot stand the sight of
blood, finds a baby girl stranded aboard an empty ship and decides to raise her.
ISBN 1-58234-866-9 (alk. paper)
[1. Pirates—Fiction. 2. Foundlings—Fiction.] I. Sam Hearn, ill. II. Title.
PZ7.H182658 Vi 2003
[Fic]—dc21
2002028029

First U.S. Edition 2003

Printed in Great Britain by Clays Ltd, St Ives plc

1 3 5 7 9 10 8 6 4 2

Bloomsbury USA Children's Books
175 Fifth Avenue
New York, New York 10010

For Imogen – R.H.

For TelRay and BabsMags – S.H.

Chapter 1

‘There's one thing I do not want to see,’ the Pirate Captain told the crew as the ship slipped through the dark night. 'Only one thing . . .’

He curled his lip and sucked in noisily. 'And that is . . . b . . . b . . . b . . .’

The crew waited. Several of them tilted their heads to one side. They knew what he was trying to say. But could he say it?

‘B . . . b . . . b . . .’ went the Captain. His face grew red, his eyes grew wild.

The crew looked at their feet. They studied the sails above them. They peered into the dirty ears of the pirate in front. They did not want to laugh. If they laughed, the Pirate Captain might explode with fury and they were frightened of that. So they waited as the Captain worked himself up to THE WORD. He took a deep breath and tugged his beard.

'This is a raid. We sail up abroadsides and board 'em. We capture the crew and passengers. You can pull their noses. You can twist their arms. You can stamp on their toes. You can tickle 'em, steal all their things. You can be rude and 'orrible and disgusting, but I don't want to see any b . . . b . . .'

'Blindfolds?' suggested a voice. 'Backflips?'

'BLOOD!' spluttered the Captain. 'I can't stand the sight of BLOOD!' His wild eyes swept across them. There was silence.

'Oh. All right, then,' squeaked a pirate at the back.

The Pirate Captain glared at the crew's faces. Were they laughing at him? 'Take your positions!' he barked. He felt better now that he had said THE WORD.

Creaking gently, the little ship glided through the water. A light breath of wind filled the sails. Ahead they could see the outline of the cutter. It was a big ship, much bigger than theirs. The passengers, if there were any, would be asleep on board. One, maybe two sailors would be on watch. The ship was easy pickings.

'Come on my beauty,' urged the Pirate Captain to his sailing ship. 'Only a few lengths more. Then food, victuals – treasure will be ours.' He looked up at the stars. 'Please may we have some treasure?' he pleaded.

They had been watching the cutter for a whole afternoon, keeping her just in sight as they tacked back and forth across the sea. Now they were making their move. In the dead of night they would sail alongside and surprise her.

And suddenly they were there.

One ...

Two ...

Three ...

'At 'em, lads!' roared the Pirate Captain.

A hail of grappling-irons flew across the gap between the ships. They fell upon the deck and snagged in the rigging. The two ships crashed together and shuddered.

'AAAGGGHHH!'

Shouting and screaming, hollering and baying like wild animals, the pirates boarded the vessel. Some clambered up the sides with knives clenched between their teeth. Others swung in from the rigging, landing lightly, like cats, on the deck.

There they crouched, ready to spring, a knife in each hand. They looked and listened, and looked again . . . One by one the pirates fell silent.

Where was everybody?

Slowly, they took in the ship around them. The helm was tied down. The sails hung limp. A door banged. The ship was in the grip of silence.

The ship was empty.

'It's empty,' said Franklin, stating the obvious. He was a tall gangly pirate with long black hair and a gold tooth.

'Might be as they are hiding somewhere,' said a second pirate, called Gregory. He looked at a sea chest suspiciously.

'Might be,' another one piped up, 'might be one of them ghost ships, that do not have people on board but only spirits.' He was a nervous pirate, called Percy. He had little twitchy eyes, like a rabbit.

'Whaaaaat,' came the Captain's enraged whisper from below in the little pirate ship, 'whaaat, in the name of Neptune, is goin' on up thar?' He popped his head over the gunwale. His eyes darted left and right.

'It's empty, Captain, there's no one on board.'

'Empty? Empty?' the Pirate Captain repeated. 'Careful my laddies – this could be a trick. I reckon they is 'ere somewhere. They is just waiting to spring upon us and frighten the life out of us.' He climbed carefully on to the deck. He peered into the corners, into the shadows. Maybe the ship's crew had seen them coming and were waiting to ambush them. He looked at the door that led below. Maybe they were there.

'Frankie – you lead the way below decks. I'll follow with Percy and Gregory at the rear.'

They found a lantern and, taking their places in a little line, the four pirates stepped through the galley door, which led immediately down some steep steps, into the hull of the ship.

Chapter 2

Ahead of them the lantern light flickered over the wooden beams and panels. Franklin swung the lantern from side to side and shadows danced around them.

What a mess! There were clothes and bottles and cups and papers lying everywhere. There was broken furniture, open chests and split barrels in heaps.

'Whoa! What a messy lot!' whispered Franklin, his gold tooth glinting in the lantern light.

'It's like Greg's cabin,' said Percy, peeping from behind the Captain.

'Shut up, the pair of you,' growled the Captain. 'They might jump on us any minute.' The Captain was uneasy – he'd seen mess like this somewhere before. There had been a fight here, no doubt about it.

They crept in single file along a passage then down some more steps. Now they were in the sleeping quarters. Hammocks swung from the ceiling, clothes lay scattered on the deck, spilling out of chests.

'Slovenly lot!' tutted Franklin, holding up the lantern.

'I fink it's a nice mess,' countered Gregory from the back. 'Actually, I could be quite at home here.'

'Shhhh,' the Captain snarled.

They picked their way through the sleeping

quarters, stepping over the scattered clothes and watching the shadows for a tell-tale glint of silver. Beyond, lay the dining area. Two long tables stretched down the middle of the room. There were chairs and benches overturned. The remains of a meal lay on the tables – dirty plates and jugs and pewter cups. Franklin lifted the lantern: 'Rats!' he squawked, and they just had time to see a dozen black rodents frozen in the light – before he dropped the lantern and plunged them into darkness.

'You blithering idiot!' swore the Captain. 'You ham-fisted, butter-fingered, bread-headed poop of a pirate!'

'Shhh.' Gregory gripped the Captain's arm. They listened.

'I don't hear nothing,' said Franklin.

'I heard somefink. Like a pussycat.'

'It's the rats . . .'

'It's spirits,' wailed Percy. 'I am a-tingling all over. Me hairs are standing up.'

'Tell 'em to sit down again,' growled the Captain. 'An' relight the blinking lantern.'

Franklin struck a match and relit the lantern. The rats scurried into dark corners. 'Why has nobody cleared up?' he asked, bothered.

'Maybe they liked it that way,' said Gregory.

'Maybe they abandoned ship 'cos there was an 'orrible disease on board,' suggested Percy.

'Maybe,' said the Captain, thinking hard, 'maybe there was some pirates here.'

'You mean we is raiding a pirate ship?' Percy gulped.

'No. You barnacle brain! I mean – yes, in a way we are.' The Pirate Captain suddenly grinned at them. 'This ship 'as already *been* raided. That's why it is in such a terrible and disgusting mess. This is the way *we* usually leave a ship after *we've* raided it. That is why all the barrels and chests are overturned and empty. Why there is no people on board – they 'ave all walked the plank or been chucked overboard. Why—'

He stopped. The other pirates looked at him. He listened. In the lamplight, his eyebrows twitched quizzically.

Then everyone heard it. A cry.

Slowly, silently, with their hearts thumping, the pirates crept through the dining-room towards the noise. It came from a cabin at the end of a passage. A light shone from underneath the door.

At the count of three, the four pirates burst in.

They had knives and pistols at the ready. Two of them tripped over a chair and flew headlong into a bunk. The next two fell on top of them. Looking up, they heard a little gurgle of laughter.

Sitting in bed was a baby.

It was smiling at them.

Chapter 3

'It's a baby,' said Franklin, stating the obvious.
'I can see that,' said the Pirate Captain. 'Get
orf my leg.'

''Ere, let me see. I've never seen a baby,' said
Gregory, pushing forward to get a better look.
'Eee. It's very small,' he said, sounding
disappointed.

'Nah – that's a big baby. 'E is sitting up and
playing,' said Percy. 'Little babies can't even sit up.'

'Since when did you know so much, Mother
Percy?' sneered Franklin.

'I have ten brothers and sisters,' Percy said, 'an' I'm
the eldest. I wasn't always a pirate, y'know.'

'Stop this clucking,' spluttered the Captain.

'Think. What is this baby doing here? Why is a baby sitting on a ship all alone? It ain't right.'

'It's a nice baby,' said Gregory.

'It doesn't matter that the baby is nice – what's it doing here? With the light on? It wasn't reading a book!'

The pirates thought. The baby had obviously been left by someone, but . . . Franklin caught sight of something in the baby's bed.

'What's that?' he asked.

It was a note. The pirates stared at it.

we av fed everrybodi
to the sHarks
but we cannt kil
the Babe.
Luk after it.
PLese.

'Must be foreigners,' sniffed the Captain, after looking hard at it for a while.

'I fink it's Portuguese,' said Franklin.

'Let's get Corky – he can read,' suggested Gregory.

But the Pirate Captain snatched the note from Franklin and peered at it again. He didn't like the suggestion that he couldn't read. It undermined his authority. To think that the ship's cook could read and the Pirate Captain couldn't. It was insulting! He looked at it the right way up and then he looked at it upside-down.

'Terrible 'andwriting,' he told them. 'Can't possibly read it. It's what they call "illegible".' He lowered his voice. 'I fink this could be . . . a trap.'

He looked at the baby as if it were a ticking bomb. The baby beamed back at him. 'Pick him up,' he ordered, 'an' bring him with us. At least we got a captive!'

'Take the baby?' said Franklin in disbelief.

'Yeah,' the Pirate Captain glowered at him.

'Aye, aye, Captain,' Franklin muttered. The baby gurgled delightedly when Percy picked it up. He wiped its little nose with the filthy spotted handkerchief around his neck. It made happy, contented noises as they carried it to the bows of the ship. Percy shushed it to keep it quiet. Papers and bottles and broken furniture lay strewn about.

'They is gorn,' said Franklin looking at the mess.

'All gorn. Taken everyfink. An' left us holding the baby,' agreed the Captain grumpily.

''Dah,' said the baby, smiling at the rough pirates.

As they climbed up the fore steps and emerged on to the open deck, dawn was breaking. The other pirates gathered around and looked at the baby.

An enormous pirate called Big Bron pushed his way to the front and stared at the baby.

'Arrrrr,' he said. He put his huge tar-blackened hand out – it was almost as big as the baby itself. 'Cooocheeee coooooooooo!' he said in a great deep voice, and prodded the baby with a thick finger.

'Careful, Bron,' squeaked Percy. 'This is a baby, not a lump o' cheese.'

'I is as careful as a butterfly,' growled Big Bron, giving Percy a frightening look.

'That is one mighty fine and beautiful baby,' chirped Corky the cook, coming between them. He was a little round pirate with twinkling blue

eyes and a stripy bandanna. Instead of a cutlass, he had a long spoon tucked into his belt. 'Why, 'tis many a year since I seen such a little ''un. An' so round and pretty too! Just look at his little fingers – aren't they just as eency-weency as a leprechaun's. And his eyes – as emerald as the fair isle itself . . .'

'Hey! Corky! Come 'ere!' ordered the Pirate Captain, beckoning with his finger.

He showed him the note they had found with the baby. 'Course the writing is terrible,' he warned conspiratorially, 'and the spelling quite villainous . . . but maybe . . . together we could . . .'

'Read it, Captain? Aye, aye, sir,' said Corky quietly. He took out some little gold spectacles and peered at the writing. Very softly he read into the Pirate Captain's ear:

we av fed everrybodi to the sharks but we cannt kil the Babe. Luk after it plese.

'They 'as all been fed to the sharks,' cried the Pirate Captain, snatching the paper. 'I 'as read the rotten note left by that wicked gang o' buccaneers! They 'as stolen every brass knob on the ship – an' left a baby! Heartless buzzards!'

'Arrr, that means he is an orphan,' said Corky, looking fondly at the baby.

'What's an orphan?' Gregory asked.

'Means he's got no mum and dad,' said Percy.

'If those scoundrels had one grain of honour, they would have fed this baby to the sharks too!' said the Captain.

'W . . . w . . . why's that?' asked Percy.

The Captain explained. 'Which would you like: to be left to drift about in a ship, dying of 'unger? Or die quick an' easy with the sharks?'

'Or end up being found by mean and rotten pirates?' added Franklin with a frightening grin.

'Hey, that's not so bad,' cried Corky. 'Maybe we *are* a bit rough, but we've saved him, like good Christians. The baby has no mum and dad – to be sure, we could look after him!'

'Don't be ridicculus,' growled the Pirate Captain.

'Look after a baby?' sneered Franklin. He spat over the side of the ship in disgust.

There were cries of 'Pah!' and 'Barmy!' from the other pirates.

'Why not?' said Percy.

There was a pause while they all thought. The Pirate Captain decided to keep quiet. Let them work it out for themselves, he thought. He walked over to the side of the ship. He watched the dawn sun slowly rising in the sky and picked his teeth.

Franklin spoke. 'Well. Babies need fings. Like cots and prams and fings.'

'We can make cots and prams,' said Percy.

'An' they need special food.'

'I can make special food,' said Corky. 'I could feed him mashed biscuits and weevils and he'd be as big as Bron in a week!'

'Babies are dreadful messy,' said Franklin, shaking his head.

'I don't mind,' smiled Gregory.

'They need . . . ' the Pirate Captain began coolly,

then spun around. 'NAPPIES! Anyone thought o' that?'

There was silence. The pirates frowned. They frowned all together – a big group frown. It felt as if a cloud had passed over the sun.

Then Big Bron spoke. 'I'll ... make ... some ... nappies.'

The pirates were stunned. Big Bron was looking fondly at the baby. The baby was gazing back.

The Pirate Captain practically swallowed his toothpick. He spat it out, on deck.

'I cannot ... ever, ever, no – not in a million years – ever ... have n ... n ... n ... *nappies* swinging from the yardarm. Keep the baby? Have n ... n ... nappies drying ... next to ... the Jolly Roger? The sacred skull and crossbones!'

'No, sir,' said Corky quickly. 'No need to worry. I shall dry 'em on the stove.'

'You will?' asked the Captain, with a mixture of relief and horror.

'Yes, sir. He can eat in there and sleep in the pantry. It'll be awful cosy so it will.'

The Pirate Captain was speechless. He needed time to think. 'Let's have a cup o' tea, lads, then search the ship. We came for victuals and treasure. And victuals and treasure we must find. I know there's been pirates here before us but maybe they is pirates who has missed something. They've left a baby – maybe they've left something else. We must take a proper look. Fetch anything that is worth

anything. Knock on every panel, open every cupboard. Sniff out the secret compartments – every ship 'as 'em. Once that is done . . . then we shall think about the baby. Eh?'

The pirates agreed and set about searching the ship. They went down into the hold and brought out sails and buckets, plates and jugs, ropes and a set of carpenter's tools. There was a broken clock, a pile of clothes, the head and leg of a suit of armour. They found half a barrel of stinking salted beef in the kitchens and a couple of kegs of gunpowder in the hold.

Percy and Corky brought out the baby things. There was a cot, a chest full of small clothes and a rag doll.

The Pirate Captain slouched on a sail chest, looking more and more grumpy as each thing came out. No grub, no treasure. Just a baby and a heap of clothes. Not a stick of decent furniture. He gazed out at the sea, drinking tea. Maybe he should have done something else with his life – become a lighthouse keeper or a goldsmith perhaps. If he'd been a goldsmith he could have gazed at treasure all day long . . .

'That's the lot, Captain,' Franklin told him, dumping a sea chest on the deck.

The men gathered round.

'This is it? This?' The Pirate Captain hauled himself up and sourly inspected the booty. He lifted a cloth here, tapped a chest there. ''Ave you checked *every* cupboard? 'Ave you looked for false bottoms an' secret compartments?'

'Yeah,' said the men. The Captain always asked the same questions. They always gave the same answers.

'An' this is the baby stuff, eh?' he said, coming to the pile from the baby's cabin. He looked at the cot, swinging gently with the ship. He wasn't about to have that on board. He turned away.

But then . . . *something* about it caught his eye – something odd. The depth maybe? He lifted the blankets, then the straw mattress – and there, jumping out at him, as clear as daylight to the practised piratical eye – was an outline. The outline of a secret compartment!

He looked at his men, and they saw the gleam of excitement dancing in his eyes.

The pirates jumped up and started towards him.

'Stand back,' he snarled roughly, snatching a dagger from his belt. He looked at the baby in

Percy's arms and made a promise to himself. If . . .
If only . . . If there is hidden treasure in the baby's
cot – then – *I will keep the baby.*

Carefully, he prised the lid of the compartment
off. Inside lay a casket. The Pirate Captain gently
slid it out and held it high.

A shout went up, a triumphant cheer – so loud
that it frightened the small baby and it cried for the
first time – only in their excitement the pirates
didn't hear it.

The Captain opened the casket, and grinned wickedly. There were jewels – not many, but enough. Enough to share out. Enough to put towards their future. To add to each man's little stash.

He felt he had a vision of the future, and the baby was there, at the centre of everything.

He closed the casket and swaggered over to the baby. He put the casket down and took the baby for the first time. 'This baby,' he told everyone softly, 'is a lucky baby. 'E is a lucky mascot. 'E 'as brought us a little bit o' wealth. 'E 'as, you could say, paid his passage – and handsomely.' His voice rose. 'Shall we vote on keepin' 'im, and bringin' 'im up to be a mean and rotten pirate like us?'

'Aye!' they agreed.

'Now say 'Aye' again, if you're for keepin' our little mascot!' he cried.

'AYE!' they shouted.

The Pirate Captain held the baby aloft, and kissed it.

Chapter 4

The baby began by giving the pirates a surprise. They had loaded the booty on to the *Sleek Sally* – their little sailing ship – and cast off from the cutter, leaving her to drift on the ocean. They didn't want such a big ship, she was too slow and could be seen too easily.

They stored the booty, and had a cooked breakfast of fried salt beef and biscuits washed down with mugs of tea. They were settling down to a lazy day, lying in the sun, mending sails and sharpening fishhooks, when a cry went up in the galley.

Moments later Percy appeared, in a fluster.

'The baby!' he panted. 'The baby – it's a girl!'

'The baby is a girl?' repeated Franklin.

'I thought 'e was a boy,' said Gregory, mystified. 'How can 'e be a girl?'

No one bothered to answer that question.

'What's that?' groaned the Pirate Captain above them. He was lying in his hammock on the poop deck with his hat over his face to keep the sun off. Now he put his hands over the hat. He could weep. A girl? A girl pirate on his ship?

But he had made a promise and he was a man of his word. And maybe she was lucky? He knew some lady pirates. Kate Creole. Musket Molly. They were bad, wicked, worse than the men pirates, some said. He removed the hat, wiped his brow with his dirty sleeve.

'So what, if he is a girl?' he asked wearily.

Percy was silent. His nose twitched.

'Can't 'ave girls on board!' muttered a voice.

'Girls is trouble,' coughed Gregory.

'They's unlucky,' said Big Bron.

'Frightened of 'em, are you?' the Captain asked. 'Worried she'll show you up?'

'Not us!' said the pirates.

'Good,' replied the Pirate Captain stroking his beard. He made an announcement: 'We shall call 'er Violet. After my mum!'

'Or Vile, for short,' suggested Gregory.

'And here she is!' cried Corky, appearing from below. 'All washed and dressed and fed and ready to play!' He held Violet proudly, to show her off – the little pirate baby. She had a red bandanna and little purple trousers and around her waist a green cummerbund.

'Very comely,' grumbled the Captain, and lay back in his hammock. He was not going to get all soppy about a baby. That would set a bad example.

Corky put her down on the deck. Their new responsibility. Violet stood on her feet, holding his thick fingers above her. She was smiling. 'This little babe,' Corky told the crew, 'is not really a babe at all: she is, in fact, a toddler! Although her little legs have been on the land and aren't yet accustomed to the sea swell . . .'

He let go of her hands and all at once Violet lurched forward and ran six quick little steps straight down the sloping deck towards Big Bron.

As she reached him, she toppled over and launched herself head first into the big man's stomach.

'Arrrrgh!' he cried, surprised and winded. 'Your 'ead – is – like – a – cannonball! Heh, heh!'

He picked her up, popped her on her feet again and set her off like a toy running back across the deck.

'Wheeee!' she went as she lurched towards Franklin. One by one the pirates caught her and

sent her back. Each time she crossed the deck, she laughed so much that it started the pirates laughing too.

There was something about Violet's happiness that spread through the crew. Maybe this was what they needed, a child to play with, to cheer them up on their long sea voyages.

There was a fresh salty wind and a strong sun and they'd found jewels and a baby.

Life was good.

Corky took Violet to each of the pirates and introduced her.

'This is Franklin. He's the first mate.'

'Fank,' said Violet. The pirates laughed.

'This is Gregory.'

'Egg,' she said.

'This is Big Bron.'

'Pig pong,' she managed, then beamed at all the laughing men.

'Reckon I'd better take you on a tour of the ship before we get into trouble,' said Corky, winking.

'Pig pong!' said Violet again, hopping on her little feet and hoping for the same reaction.

Corky helped her along the gangway and up the

steps to the poop deck. The Pirate Captain was snoring now. It had been a long night and the warm sun and fresh wind was delicious. As Violet approached, there was a gust of wind and the ship suddenly lurched. She toppled forward, flailing in the air for support. Her hands fell on the Pirate

Captain's red beard and she grabbed hold of it. The next moment another gust of wind hit them and her feet were lifted clean off the deck so that she was swinging on the beard.

'WWHHHHHHHHOOOOOOOA . . .'

The Pirate Captain woke with a baby swinging on his beard. It hurt like a thousand needles stabbing his jaw. He fell out of his hammock almost on top of the baby, and clutched his face.

'You barnacle-brained baboon! You are . . . SHARK FOOD!' he cried, immediately losing his temper. He picked Violet up, disentangled her little hands from his beard and, holding her high over his head, prepared to throw her overboard.

'Stop!' cried Corky. 'She didn't mean it!'

'Baaah!' the Pirate Captain stopped. The ship righted itself as the gust passed. He looked at the little baby. Violet was frightened — her bottom lip trembled but still she looked him straight in the eye. ''Tis a terrible thing to pull a sleeping pirate's beard,' he told her, putting his face up to hers. 'Do it again an' I chop you up and feed you bit by bit to the fishes!' he warned.

'Pig? Pong?' said Violet quietly.

'Eh? You cheeky nipper!' he said surprised.

He couldn't help a little smile. He looked at Corky. 'You better teach 'er some manners, eh, Corky?'

'Aye, Captain,' said Corky, taking Violet from the Captain. 'Some piratical manners, I should reckon.'

The Pirate Captain smiled. 'Start her training right away. How to become a mean and rotten pirate. Lesson one.'

Chapter 5

Lesson one, they all decided, was to get to know every inch of the ship.

The *Sleek Sally* was old and battered, but she was fast. For a pirate ship that needed to sneak up on the big galleons, speed was crucial.

'That's the mainmast, the mizzenmast, the foremast, the stern, the bow, the wheel, the poop deck, the main deck, the bee seat, the crow's nest.'

Every day for a year the pirates named the parts of the ship until Violet knew her binnacle from her bowsprit, her port from her starboard.

She found her sea legs too. Soon she was running across the decks skipping over ropes, dodging the cups of tea that the pirates had a habit of leaving around. In a few months she was jumping down hatches and playing tag between the deck stanchions.

She didn't just find her sea legs either – she found her sea bottom. Whenever the waves were high and the *Sleek Sally* pitched and tossed on the sea swell, Violet gave up walking (or rather reeling from side to side) and slid on her bottom instead. With Big Bron's tough canvas shorts protecting her from splinters, she shot around the ship like a bobsleigh.

'Cup o' tea for the helm,' Corky would cry from the galley, and in a series of daring slides, Violet would deliver the tea to the helmsman – and though the cup wasn't exactly full (and sometimes there was a deal of sea water in it too), the helmsman was delighted to have it.

Lesson two was to learn the ship's day. Franklin explained it to her:
 'We get up
 'ave a cup o' tea
 Then breakfast
 'ave a cup o' tea
 Then lunch
 'ave a cup o' tea

Then supper
'ave a cup o' tea
Then we go to bed.'
'With a cup o' tea,' said Violet.

Food – or victuals as they called it – was as much on the pirates' mind as treasure, and Violet looked forward to mealtimes.

When she was about two years old, they built Violet a high chair so she could sit and eat at the table. She learned to grab her food and gobble it down quick before someone else started eyeing it. She learned not to look too closely at what she was eating (she might see the worms and the weevils). Instead, she learned to feel a cockroach with her tongue and spit it out directly with an oath.

'BLAST THE BUG!' she'd shout, then spit it out and squish it with her fist.

Whenever that happened, the pirates banged the table and roared with laughter. They loved the sight of their little girl pirate and her piratical ways.

Lesson three was learning to go to sleep as the ship rocked and the pirates sang sea shanties up above.

Violet was soon too big for the cot, and when she was three years old, the pirates built her a little cabin of her own. It had a bunk with steps up to it and a porthole behind. They made a curtain to hang across the bed and hung a bell outside so that

she could ring if she needed anything. Percy knitted her a teddy bear and Big Bron made a canvas doll. She lay there at night listening to Gregory's accordion playing soft sea songs, and when the moon was out she gazed at the silvery sea and watched the birds following the ship.

Growing up at sea was very different from growing up on land. Violet didn't know about trees and flowers and rabbits, but she knew about the wind and the sea, about flying fish and dolphins. She couldn't read or write, but she could tie knots and spit. She never had a bedtime, just went to bed when she wanted, and like all the other pirates, she hardly ever bothered with a bath.

Then, when they judged she was old enough, they gave her a knife. This was lesson four.

'First of all it's fer eating wiv,' said Franklin. 'Slice the bread and shove it in, like this.'

'Don't you cut yer tongue?' asked Violet.

'Bah! I is a pirate. I is used to it!' Franklin laughed.

'Next,' said Corky, 'it's a grand blade for peeling spuds. It's a splendid spoon for stirring cups o' tea and guess what — a fabulous fork for feeding yourself chunks o' fish . . .'

'It's fer fightin' wiv,' snarled Franklin play-acting.

'It's fer playin' games wiv,' said Gregory spinning the knife through the air so it struck — thunk! — in the wall behind.

'An' it's for whittlin' wood when you're bored,' said Percy.

Violet took the knife.

And immediately cut her finger.

'Don't show the Captain!' cried Corky.

'Why?' asked Violet.

'Can't stand the sight o' blood!' whispered Gregory, rolling his eyes.

They bound the wound and tucked the little knife in a sheath in Violet's cummerbund.

'How can you be a pirate an' not like the sight o' blood?' asked Violet. 'If you're on a raid ain't there lots of blood?'

'Pints of it!' said Franklin.

'Gallons!' laughed Gregory.

'Well, what happens to the Captain?'

''E never looks,' they said frowning. ''E averts 'is eyes, 'cos 'e is a-feared of what will happen.'

'Truth is,' Percy explained in his jittery voice, 'all the silverware – them swords and knives and suchlike – is mostly fer show! We frighten people, but don't actually use it, unless we 'ave to!'

''Ang on. When we is attacked, then we is fearsome – is we not?' said Gregory, affronted. 'I 'as seen Mr Franklin run three fellas through like a kebab!'

'Yeah, with little onions in between!'

'An' Gregory, you 'as sliced a man in two!'

'In two?' cried Violet. 'Straight down the middle?'

'Terrible messy,' tutted Franklin.

'Well,' admitted Gregory, 'I did chop 'is finger clean orf, so 'e was then in two pieces!'

Lesson five was learning how to sail the *Sleek Sally*. Violet learned to spin the helm to move the rudder and change direction. She learned to watch the wind in the sails to keep them tight and not let them flap uselessly. She learned to scramble up the rigging to the sails, to haul in the great canvas sheets or unfurl them. She could run, sure-footed as a monkey, along the yards high up in the ship's rigging.

As she grew up, the rigging became her special place. The pirates made her a rope swing so she could swing between the masts. Afterwards, she would sit for hours in the crow's nest at the top of the main mast, gazing out at the sea spread out around her. She loved the sea, she loved to watch it glitter in the sunshine or grow dark and dangerous in the low, black suffocating skies before a storm.

From the crow's nest she watched the pirates going about their business on the deck far below. As time passed, Violet's world – the only world she knew – remained the ship and the sea and the pirates who had saved her. Land to her was a distant smudge on the horizon. They simply never went there.

Growing up with them, she became one of them in every way. Her clothes were patched. Her skin was burnt by the sun and the salt sea wind. Her fair hair was tied by a scarf. She did everything they did. She stitched sails, scrubbed the decks, and peeled potatoes in the galley till her hands were raw.

The Pirate Captain taught her to navigate by the stars. Franklin taught her how to read the wind. Big Bron spent hours with her in the bows of the ship, watching dolphins and seabirds as the ship sliced through the dark water.

Whenever anyone had a birthday, the pirates put on a show. There'd be dancing and singing. They held eating competitions and knife-throwing competitions and juggling competitions. As they didn't know Violet's birthday, they celebrated the day that they had saved her instead. Then they put on the funniest show they could. Franklin and Corky dressed up as clowns and hit each other with fish. Big Bron became a fire-eater who kept burning his beard. Gregory lay on a hammock of nails and pretended to hurt himself. And their little Violet screamed with laughter. Finally, the Pirate Captain appeared with an enormous cake that he had cooked himself. It was her favourite evening of the year, and it became the pirates' favourite evening too.

For the pirates loved her, their little Pirate Princess, and she loved them just as much. They would do anything for her and she would do anything for them. Only one thing was forbidden.

Until she was eight years old, Violet was not allowed to take part in a raid. Every time they raided another ship, they locked her up.

Chapter 6

That was the worst time for Violet. Locked up in her cabin, she could only listen to the raid happening above her. She heard the cries and shouts, the boom of ships colliding, the clash of swords, the groans of wounded men. Sometimes she heard the splashes as people jumped overboard.

But she was never sure if the pirates were winning or losing a fight. Was that cry one of her pirates? Or one of the other crew? She only knew if the raid was swift and easy or long and hard.

The easy raids were quiet.

The pirates boarded the ship and began discussions. They'd ask for food and drink, then treasure. Money, gold and jewellery to add to their stash.

She often heard the Pirate Captain shouting commands.

'Hand over everything – or we'll slit yer throats. We'll slice you from your nose to your toes!'

He sounded so fearsome, and sitting in her cabin below Violet herself would have been frightened, if it weren't for the fact that she knew slicing up the captives was the *last* thing the Pirate Captain would ever do! Think of the b . . . b . . . b . . .

Treasure, treasure, treasure. After victuals, that was all the pirates wanted. They prayed for it. They dreamed of it. But they didn't find much. A purse of money here. A pretty necklace there. A ring from someone's finger. Surely some day they would find a whole chest stuffed full of treasure, a whole ship sparkling and glittering as it sailed across the sea?

The Pirate Captain grew bad-tempered and out of sorts. The crew grumbled that his luck was bad.

From her little porthole Violet gazed at the sea and sky and listened to the raids. Until one day at dawn, the pirates boarded a ship and Violet's porthole was directly opposite another porthole.

To her surprise she found she was gazing directly into another cabin.

She could see a man rushing around in the other ship frantically hiding things. He was stuffing them into a secret compartment in the floor. He closed it, turned around and saw Violet.

Their eyes met. Violet's heart leapt. His dark eyes were alive with panic.

He glanced at the floorboard he had just replaced and back at Violet. He was tall and thin and dressed

in the cleanest clothes Violet had ever seen. She saw his smooth shaved face, his white hands with polished nails like pearls.

'You're one of them,' he said slowly and reached for something by the bunk.

Suddenly he pulled a sword from its scabbard and

lunged at Violet's porthole. The blade went through the porthole, between the ships, and through into Violet's cabin, narrowly missing her eye.

Quick as a cat, she rolled off the bunk and the sword withdrew. Then it plunged in again. The man was trying to reach further into her cabin.

The long silver blade stabbed the beams and cut into the bunk. It swept lethally through the air at head height. Violet shrank into the corner as still more of the blade came in, followed by the white hand and the pearly fingernails. The man was now at full stretch, slashing blindly, up and down, side to side. If he reached in any further he would cut her.

She pulled at the cabin door. It was locked. There was no escape.

The man couldn't see her — that was good. She ducked past the sword and climbed on to the bunk. In a moment she was next to the hand, looking at the wrist twisting and stabbing around the cabin.

Without thinking, she bit the hand, sinking her teeth hard into the clean white skin.

There was a high-pitched yelp from the other ship and the hand withdrew, dropping the sword on to the bed.

A moment later, another noise came from the

other cabin: Gregory was in there fighting the man. There was a grunt or two and a piratical roar and Gregory's face appeared in the porthole.

'You all right, Vile?' he asked.

Violet looked out. 'I bit 'im,' she said grinning.

'Nearly took his hand orf!' exclaimed Gregory.

'He tried to hurt me!' said Violet, shaking.

'That were jolly bad of 'im,' said Gregory lightly. He was searching the cabin. 'Why did 'e want to do a fing like that?'

''Cos I saw him hiding stuff!' Violet told him.

'Did you, my beauty?' Gregory put his face up to the porthole. His black eyes glinted. 'An' where would that be – his little hiding-place?'

'In the floor by the bed. Those boards come up.'

'So they do,' Gregory chuckled as he loosened the boards and pulled them up. He took out a leather purse. Eyes sparkling, he held up a gold coin. He put it in the corner of his mouth – where his three remaining teeth were – gave it a bite and winced with pain. 'It ain't chocolate!' he said gleefully.

Chapter 7

At mid-morning tea, the Pirate Captain came on deck and called a meeting. It was time to share out the spoils. From the crow's nest Violet watched the pirates gather round. The Captain sat at a little gilded French table. He looked at the pirates in front of him and then slowly raised his eyes, up the mast, through the sails, to the little figure in the crow's nest. He was looking directly at Violet. All the pirates' eyes followed the Captain's gaze.

'You too, Violet,' he called.

Violet climbed out, a little surge of excitement trembling through her. She swung across on her little swing and slid down the mast to the deck.

The Captain made her stand at the front as he split the treasure into piles. One for each pirate. Then he called their names and they each took their little pile of treasure. When it was Violet's turn she stepped forward and the Pirate Captain pushed her share towards her. There were three gold coins and a pair of earrings. And a small enamel box.

'Well done, Violet,' he said softly, and winked.

Smiling with pleasure, Violet took her booty. She went down to her cabin and gazed at it in private. The gold coins were shiny and yellow, each with a head on one side and a bird on the other. The earrings were also gold, set with a green stone you could see into. She liked them, but not just because they were beautiful – she liked them because it meant that she was an equal now.

'Keep your stash safe,' Corky told her in the galley later. 'And don't tell a soul where you're keeping it. I shouldn't say it, but there's some pirates would thieve it as soon as look at you.'

'I know treasure is nice to look at,' Violet said, 'but what's it *for*?'

'A rainy day,' said Corky spooning tea leaves into a huge teapot.

'Why do you want treasure on a rainy day?' Violet asked.

Corky laughed. 'When there's trouble around, it's good to have money to help you through it. Treasure is money. If we get enough treasure we'll be able to live how we want to live. Now go and find a hiding place, before you lose it.'

Violet went back to her cabin and hid her treasure inside her straw mattress. That way she'd be able to feel it in the night and know that it was all right.

Then she went around asking each pirate what they wanted to do with their treasure. How did they really want to live?

Franklin wanted to buy his own boat and live on it with a nice woman.

Gregory said he wanted to run a tavern. He

would sit behind the bar serving customers beer and chatting all day.

Percy wanted to send the money home to his mum and sisters, and give them a big house.

Big Bron dreamed of keeping pigs. He'd name each of them after a sea that he'd sailed in.

She couldn't help noticing that none of them said they wanted to be pirates . . . She climbed the rigging and sat in the crow's nest and thought.

What did *she* want treasure for? She didn't think she wanted her own boat or to run a tavern. And she didn't have a mum or brothers and sisters. She might want to keep pigs. (They had captured a pig once and kept it on board, feeding it scraps. And it was very friendly to her and Big Bron. Unfortunately, it bit the Captain and they had to put it in the pot.)

No, Violet thought she was really quite happy being a pirate. And anyway she couldn't think what else she could be. What else did she know? She'd never even seen inside any of the other ships. She'd never set foot on land.

She climbed out of the crow's nest and took hold of the rope swing that the pirates had rigged up for her. She held on to the baton of wood and swung in a great arc above the deck to a platform on another mast. There was another swing there and she set it swinging and moved expertly between the two, letting go of one as the other magically arrived for her to grasp.

Below, the pirates watched. They never ceased to marvel at the perfect timing and natural grace Violet possessed. Occasionally, they all gasped, thinking she might fall and hurt herself.

'Careful, careful,' they muttered under their breath as Violet swung back and forth.

As she landed on the platform, Franklin appeared round the thick mast. 'C'mon, Violet. Time to do some fishin'. There's a shoal is just passed us.'

'Do I have to?' moaned Violet.

'Chores is chores,' said Franklin. 'C'mon, I'll race yer there.'

She swung out to the other mast, then, all in one movement, slid part way down it, caught another rope, swung out and landed exactly at the stern.

She turned back, grinning. Franklin was where she knew he'd be. Still on the platform, hands on hips, eyeing her reproachfully. He knew he didn't stand a chance in a race with Violet.

They fished for three hours and caught several
dozen gleaming mackerel. As they fished, Franklin
told stories about his time on other pirate ships.
He'd been on three before this one and they were
hard and rough – not like this ship at all. He liked
this ship.

'Of course we is frightening pirates,' he said, 'but

underneath, some of us is pussycats,' he told her, winking.

'What's a pussycat?' asked Violet.

Franklin frowned. How could she not know what a pussycat was? That was the weird thing about Violet, he thought, because she was growing up on a ship, she didn't know about the commonest things. He tried to explain. 'It's a sort of small furry thing, like a rat . . . but bigger and cuddly-like.'

Violet tried to imagine it. Wrongly, as it later turned out.

They took the mackerel to Corky in the galley. Violet helped as he gutted and fried them for lunch. He threw them into a big frying pan where they sizzled and spat. After a minute or two Violet scooped them out with a big slatted spoon. She put them on a tray and took them through to the dining area. The pirates helped themselves with their fingers, piling fish on to their plates.

There were plenty of sucking noises and smacking of lips and a few complaints about the bones, but it was a good meal and they were soon satisfied.

When he finished, the Pirate Captain stood up

and made Violet stand next to him. 'As Captain o'
the *Sleek Sally*,' he said, 'I would like to say well
done again to little Violet for finding them jewels
in that fella's cabin,' he said.

The pirates banged their fists on the table. 'Nice
one, Vile!' they chorused.

'I reckon you is now a fit an' proper pirate, mean and rotten to the core, and ready for raidin'! We 'as looked forward to this day for a long time, hasn't we, lads? Ever since we 'as found you on that abandoned ship.'

The pirates banged their fists on the table again. 'Come wiv me, Violet,' the Pirate Captain said solemnly, 'and we shall choose you a proper cutlass.'

Violet followed him to his cabin. She had been there many times and each time it seemed there was less and less room. The Pirate Captain had a liking for fine furniture and he stored it all in his cabin.

For he too had his dreams. 'One day,' he had told her, 'I shall have a fine house with lots of rooms filled with lovely furniture looted from ships.' He chuckled.

Violet looked around. Chairs, tables, desks and chests lay one on top of the other, quite blocking out the light from the windows.

The Pirate Captain sat down at the chart table and slurped his after-lunch tea. 'When you go on a raid,' he said, 'I expect you to behave in a truly rotten manner. We shall be tying up some nice and kind people, being very rude to them, poking 'em like a herd of naughty pigs, and taking all their chests of treasure away. Are you 'appy doing that?'

'Aye,' Violet said. 'I reckon.'

'Good.' The Pirate Captain drank from his mug and then licked his tea-stained moustache. 'As you know, there is only one rule.' He seemed troubled

and took a deep breath: 'No b . . . b . . . b . . . ' He stopped. Then quickly gabbled: 'It begins with "b" and ends with "d" an' I don't want to see any of it. There.'

Violet nodded, trying not to smile. She wondered what would happen if he did see it.

The Pirate Captain wiped his mouth on his sleeve and stood up. He took a cutlass out of the drawer. It was thin and neat, and sharp. He swished it about, bit it and peered along its length. 'Here you are,' he said handing it over. 'It's a beauty. Spanish, I reckon. Now we'll practise. You an' me, on the deck. You take a cutlass an' I'll 'ave . . . this two-handed Scottish claymore, plundered this last week from a tartan trader.' He took down from the wall a ridiculously long sword, quite as big as himself, and marched out of the cabin, up the steps on to the deck, holding it high.

Violet was about to object about the unfair size of his sword, but the Pirate Captain had already started.

'Positions. On guard! Fight!'

He roared theatrically and with an effort swung the heavy sword. Violet jumped out of the way. Struggling, the Captain held the sword vertically and parried as Violet jabbed forward this way and that.

'Get 'im, Vile,' shouted the pirates, now gathered on deck with their mugs of tea.

Violet dodged behind the mast and the Captain came after her, shouting playfully, 'I'll fillet yer, yer little ruffian.'

Violet jumped out of the way. The Captain swept the sword knee-high across the deck, and sunk it into the mast. Where it stuck fast.

AAAAARRGH!

'Get 'im, Vile,' cried the pirates.

In a second her cutlass was quivering at his heart.

'Mercy, my love,' he snarled, eyeing the blade.

Violet withdrew her sword.

'Sail!' a voice from above cried suddenly. 'Sail to the starboard!'

The Captain straightened up. 'Nice work,' he said to Violet, winking at her. Breathing heavily, he took out his telescope. In the distance he saw a dark little dot on the horizon.

'Two in one day?' he muttered with evident pleasure. 'Arr. She is a comely galleon, if ever I saw one. An' with a nice plump space for cargo, I'll be bound. English flag – so packed with riches!'

He spun round and stared at Violet. 'Are you ready?'

She nodded.

'Then this is the one for you.' Raising his voice, he cried, 'The wind is fair and she'll be on us pretty soon. Set the course, Mr Franklin! Violet, up the riggin'! Watch for yer chance and then swing in behind the others. You are second wave attack. You . . . an' me.'

Chapter 8

'Usual drill, everyone,' the Captain ordered. 'Hit 'em quick and hit 'em hard and frighten 'em rotten. Then tie 'em up and fill up on grub an' treasure. Half of everything is mine.' And please, he added to himself, in his private prayer, let there be treasure.

The galleon was coming fast towards them. They made as if to sail to starboard. Then at the last moment they changed course and tacked. When the sails settled, they had judged it just right and were only three lengths behind. What's more, they had stolen the other ship's wind so they were alongside in a jiffy.

The pirates lay hidden, then sprang up as they came alongside the other ship. They began shouting and whooping and flinging grappling-irons to tie the ships together. Violet watched as the pirates swarmed across the deck. She saw the crew of the other ship running and hiding, trying to

escape. They weren't prepared. Swords glinted in the sunlight, cries filled the air. A gun flashed and puffed out a cloud of smoke.

There was confusion, then calm. Their prey were cornered. Franklin, Gregory and Big Bron were snarling like dogs and brandishing pistols

and cutlasses at the frightened sailors. On the far side several men were down, groaning.

The Pirate Captain now strode aboard, signalling to Violet as he went. She took hold of a rope and swung aboard.

'Nice work, lads, nice work!' he cried. 'A neat little cargo ship, indeed.' He looked around. 'Where's the skipper?'

'I am the captain.' A stout little man with a red coat and a face to match pushed through. 'What's the meaning of this?' he asked angrily.

'We is pirates an' we 'as taken your ship,' replied Franklin.

'Quite so,' the Pirate Captain agreed. 'Now – we can be nice or nasty – which is it to be?'

The other captain scowled. 'What choice do I have? Either way you'll rob us.'

'Indeed we shall,' said the Pirate Captain lightly. 'Let's be nice – to start wiv. Pray tell me, what cargo do you carry?'

'Coconuts,' replied the other captain smugly.

'Coconuts?' The Pirate Captain grinned. 'And is that all?'

'Yes.'

'Come now.' His grin was fixed. 'Nobody is just

carrying coconuts. Tell me again, what other cargoes is you carrying?'

'I tell you. Only coconuts,' repeated the man.

'Don't be . . . RIDICULOUS!' barked the Pirate Captain. He leered menacingly towards the smaller man. 'No one 'as *only* coconuts.'

'I have ten thousand of them. If you don't believe me, take a look.'

The Pirate Captain gestured to Percy to have a look. 'If I find you is lying . . .' he snarled, and left the threat hanging in the air.

coconuts?

'It's full of 'em,' cried Percy, re-emerging from below decks. 'Right to the top!'

'*Coconuts?*' The Pirate Captain couldn't believe it. 'Ten thousand crummy *coconuts*. They are no blinking use. WHERE'S THE TREASURE?'

'They *are* useful actually,' corrected the other captain. 'They are amazingly useful. You can eat them. You can drink the milk. You can dry them, make oil, make soap, make rope, make doormats, make . . .'

'Pipe down, you big red jellyfish!' snarled the Pirate Captain. 'Are you thinking that I am going to spend my hours at sea making doormats? Or soap?'

The man shook his head fearfully.

'Search the cabins,' stormed the Pirate Captain. 'Turn out their pockets! Pull the rings orf of their fingers! We're gonna take every last thing from this ship. But . . . let's be nice too. An' seeing as the ten thousand nuts is so amazingly useful . . . you can keep 'em. You can eat 'em and drink 'em and dress in 'em for all I care!'

The pirates tied up the ship's crew and searched the ship. Violet went below with Gregory. The place was stuffed with coconuts. The pirates searched everywhere. They took everything that

wasn't a coconut. They took the water, the food, the clothes, the sea chests, the cooking pots, even the sailors' hammocks.

'What are these?' asked Violet, studying a bookshelf in one of the cabins.

'They is books,' said Gregory looking over.

Violet picked up one of the slim leather volumes.

'What are they for?' she asked, looking at a picture of a little girl (very oddly dressed, she thought) and a hairy animal.

'For? Vile, they ain't *for* anything! Sling 'em overboard! But first check they is not got secret compartments for jewellery. Or hasn't got paper money hidden in 'em. Some folk do hollow out the pages.'

Violet looked again at the picture. She liked it.

She wanted to know what the little girl was doing with the animal. And what was the animal saying to the little girl?

'Can I keep them?'

'Course you can. We is taking everyfink, ain't we?' Gregory said. ''Cept the coconuts!'

They piled the booty high on the *Sleek Sally*. There were chests and barrels and boxes and furniture and pictures. They didn't find any treasure, except what they managed to take from the captain and crew – a couple of gold rings and some coins.

When it was done, it was late in the afternoon and the sun was low in the sky.

They were preparing to leave when Percy grabbed the Pirate Captain's arm. He was looking over his shoulder out to sea.

'Ship!' he squeaked in horror.

The Captain looked up and there, a mile away, was a cutter in full sail bearing down on them. They had been too busy clearing the ship to watch the sea around them.

'Clear orf, get out o' here!' shouted the Captain, taken by surprise. 'That's a fighting ship, an' stuffed with weapons. Make ready the *Sally*, or we're done for!' He scrambled over the side and leapt down to the *Sleek Sally*. Leaving the crew tied up, the pirates scrambled across to their ship.

Violet shimmied up the rigging and began to unfurl the sails on their ship, ripping at the knots as fast as she could. One by one the knots came loose and the sails dropped down, flapping in the wind.

At the same time, the Pirate Captain slashed at the ropes and grappling-irons binding the *Sleek Sally* to the galleon. They had to get free fast, or there'd be trouble.

In a minute they were rolling away from the bigger ship. The stolen cargo – piled higgledy-piggledy on deck – slid across and toppled over.

Two chests tumbled into the ocean. The rest, including Violet's books, lay strewn about the deck.

Violet pulled at the ropes and more sails dropped down. The Pirate Captain grabbed the helm and the ship turned, plunging into the waves as the sails snapped taut in the brisk wind. They were off and gathering speed.

'We'll never do it,' grumbled the Captain.

Now they looked behind and saw how close the other cutter was. Half a mile at most. Half a mile and gaining.

'Come on,' the pirates urged the *Sleek Sally*.

Through his telescope the Pirate Captain could see green and white coats on the cutter. Soldiers. They would have guns and cannons.

'Pot-bellied pigs!' he swore at the top of his voice.

As he looked, he saw a puff of smoke, and ducked. A bullet whizzed past his ear. Another one thudded into the mizzenmast and there was the sound of splintering wood. A third one fell short and hit the stern.

'Piddlin' pilchards!' The Pirate Captain shook his fist in defiance at them. But it was clear that they were gaining on the *Sleek Sally*. They heard the boom of a cannon and, moments later, a splash by the side of the ship.

Violet hid behind the mast. She had seen the smoke and had heard the thud of the bullets. Some of the pirates were firing back. When she looked again she had the shock of her life: the ship was next to them.

Green-and-white coated soldiers were jumping on board the *Sleek Sally*.

Now the air was filled with cries and screams. The soldiers were fighting hand to hand with the pirates.

Violet ran up the rigging. She saw Franklin dodge a sword and fling a man overboard. Big Bron bashed two soldiers together and stuck them in a barrel. The Pirate Captain ran crazily through the mêlée, screaming like a devil and slashing at everything. In spite of this fearful scene, Violet grinned. Through the smoke she saw that the Pirate Captain's eyes were shut tight.

At the end of his run he turned and prepared to run again. Violet watched a soldier moving behind him – preparing to stab the Captain from behind. She grabbed the rope swing and without hesitating, launched herself at the man. She swooped over the deck, knocking the soldier clean overboard with her feet.

'Yessssssss!' hollered the Captain, with a warrior's gleefulness. Violet saw a wild look in his eyes, before he shut them tight, and began bashing and slashing his way through the fight and back again. When he reached the bows, he stopped. He turned around and opened his eyes. He stared.

Then Violet realised it too. The soldiers were helping their wounded comrades back. The ship was disengaging. It was sailing away.

'We've done it!' the Pirate Captain yelled. 'We've beaten 'em orf!'

The pirates fell upon each other, hugging and cheering. They danced around, jumping up and down in excitement and jeering at the ship sailing away.

'We're too much for 'em!' laughed the Pirate Captain.

'We is too terrifying!' sang Percy.

'We're the fearsomest fighters of the sea!' boasted Corky, waving a frying pan.

'We are—' began the Pirate Captain, then suddenly stopped. He looked down as if something was bothering him. He stared at his hand. His expression changed from triumph to disbelief.

His hand – it was covered in b . . . b . . . blood.

Chapter 9

The pirate crew had never seen anything like it. Not on the *Sleek Sally* and not on all the other ships they had ever served on. It was horrifying.

The Pirate Captain stared at his hand and began to wobble. Blood was dripping from the wound — yet it wasn't that bad — a few stitches would fix it.

And after all, thought Violet, what do you expect if you go charging crazily through a fight, slashing wildly with your eyes shut?

The Pirate Captain's legs suddenly buckled under him and he crumpled to the floor like an empty coat. Amazingly, he then shot up, stiff as a post, and glared at the hand as if by sheer willpower he might heal the wound.

It was crimson. The blood dripped through his fingers. 'Me h . . . h . . . hand,' he whimpered. 'They've cut it orf!' The pirates heard a snuffle. Two big tears rolled down his face, trailing into his beard.

'Mum,' said a little voice.

The pirates looked at their feet. They glanced at each other. Had he said that? Their mean and rotten Pirate Captain? The one with a voice like thunder and all them brave words? That bravado? *Mum?*

Then he crumpled again, hit the deck and lay still.

Nobody moved.

'What – did – 'e – say?' asked Big Bron incredulously.

Violet looked up at her pirates. They were big, rough, dirty men. But for a moment she imagined them as boys. Boys who loved sailing and fighting and playing games. Sure, they were rough and mean, but they were kind and soft-hearted too. And they were boys who were looking for something – not just treasure – but something else. Maybe Franklin was right: they *were* pussycats.

'Take the Captain below,' said Franklin, 'and give him a cup o' tea. Hot an' sweet an' laced wiv a tot o' rum. Ready the sail. It's getting dark an' we want to be as far away from those soldiers as possible. They'll most probably pick up the other boat and come scuttlin' after us.'

They made ready and soon the Captain was tucked up in his bunk below while the *Sleek Sally* made all speed away.

In her cabin that night, Violet opened the books she had found on the ship. There were six. Two bound in red leather and four in brown. She touched the gold letters on the front and ran her fingers over the words and pictures. She wished she could read. As it was she could only guess the story from the pictures.

There were pictures of animals and children. There were fairy queens and princes and horses and puppets. There was a little girl walking through a wood with a wolf. There were three bears and three pigs and a girl and a big hairy monster. What a strange and wonderful world it seemed.

She fell asleep with her cheek pressed against the open pages and dreamed she was the girl in the pictures.

The next morning she took one of the books to Corky as he was making the morning brew.

'Corky, can you read words?' she asked.

'Of course I can. I got me little recipe book and a little library of poems in me locker.'

'Could you read me this book?' Violet held up one of the books.

'*Fairy tales*,' read Corky, taking the book from her. 'I'd like that. Do me a favour an' take the Captain his morning brew? He has retired to his cabin an' says he won't be comin' out. I fear he has sunk into a gloom.'

Violet took the mug and walked through the ship to the Captain's cabin at the stern. She knocked on the door.

'Come in,' said a weary voice.

Violet stepped into the dark cabin, ducking round the legs of a chair that jutted out from the wall of furniture strapped to the ship's sides. The Captain was in bed, behind a worn curtain.

'Tea, Capt'n,' she said. She caught a glimpse of his eye

looking at her through a moth-hole in the curtain.

'On the table, Violet,' he said mournfully.

The fact that he didn't remind her to place it on a coaster, to protect the table from the hot tea, showed he was not well.

'Did you enjoy the raid, Violet?' he asked weakly.

'Yes, Capt'n. It was exciting,' she said.

He laughed hollowly. Then he said sourly, 'It was trouble, that ship. Coconuts and trouble. No treasure. (There's a surprise.) An' not a stick of decent furniture.'

'I got me some nice books,' said Violet.

'Books?' repeated the Captain. Two fingers lifted the curtain. The Captain looked out. He seemed changed. His eyes were tired and sad. 'You is learnin' to read?'

'Corky's gonna teach me,' said Violet.

The Captain nodded. He picked up his tea and drank it down, thirstily. He closed his eyes and breathed out heavily. Violet noticed his bandaged hand.

'Readin' is good,' he said with an effort. 'You can't be a pirate all yer life.' And so saying he dropped the curtain back down.

Chapter 10

So, with the Pirate Captain's blessing, Violet learned to read – and because she wanted to, she learned fast.

She read fairy tales and fables and myths and legends – all the stories in the six books. She read them over and over, till she knew them almost by heart.

And she became more curious than ever to go ashore and see land. She wanted to see ordinary people and houses and trees. She wanted to see a dog and a cat and a horse. She wanted to see a farm and a castle. She wanted to see other children.

Curiously, just as she started reading, the pirates stopped raiding. It seemed that the Pirate Captain had lost his stomach for a fight. A terrible change had come over him. He stayed in his cabin all day moaning and polishing his furniture. The crew were worried about him.

''E is changed from a lion into a little weasel,' said one.

''E is as tough as jelly,' sneered another.

Gregory was more thoughtful.

'Maybe 'e is ready to retire. To swap his treasure for a house and a settled life. After all, 'e can't fit no more furniture in that cabin.'

They were running out of food. If they didn't raid

a ship soon, they'd have nothing to eat, except the fish that they caught, and that was far from regular. They were growing thin, and food was rationed: a mouldy biscuit, two cups of tea and half a pint of green water a day. They began to feel weak and tired.

They were worried about Violet too.

'She's hardly speaking to me,' said Big Bron, as they lay in the shade, fishing.

'Too busy wiv them books,' grumbled Franklin, juggling with fishing floats.

'Maybe she needs something to cheer her up –

change of scene or something,' stuttered Percy, pulling up another tangle of seaweed.

At last the crew called a meeting. The Pirate Captain came with his arm in a sling and a scowl on his face. He didn't like being summoned.

Franklin put the proposal to the Captain.

'We 'as followed you a long time Captain, but—'

'We're HUNGRY,' said Gregory.

'We got nuffink to eat,' Franklin told him.

'We're gonna starve.'

'I'm orf raidin',' said the Pirate Captain grumpily. 'I don't like it any more.'

'Wot – not at all?' squeaked Percy, shocked.

'No.'

'Not even when we is hungry as horses?' asked Franklin.

'No!'

'What you going to eat, then?' demanded a voice. 'Can't eat your flippin' furniture?'

There was a snort of laughter. The Pirate Captain didn't like that. He felt angry. His face grew red. His eyes watered. As he opened his mouth to speak, a clear voice rang out. But it wasn't him, it was Violet, sitting on a platform above the pirates, swinging her legs.

'Couldn't we go and *buy* some food?'

A deathly silence fell. The Captain blinked, his mouth remained open.

'Buy?' said Franklin, as if trying out the word.

'Yes. In a town. There's shops there. I've read about it. You can pop into a shop and say, "I'll have a cabbage and a bag of carrots and some fresh meat, please." And then you pay them.'

'Pay – them?' said Big Bron.

'With money,' said Violet. The eyes of the pirates grew wider.

'Pay-them-with-money,' repeated Big Bron.

'But we is pirates,' said Franklin. 'Mean and rotten pirates. We take fings from people. We steal. We are frightening. No one is more frightening and crafty and bad than us! What's more, if the people of the town see a shipful of pilfering pirates arriving, they is going to round us up and lock us in a prison!'

'Wait a minute, lads,' said the Pirate Captain, stroking his beard. 'I got an idea. We go in disguise. We shave orf our beards – we 'ave a little 'aircut; put on some clean clothes, and not look like pirates at all!' He grinned at them.

The pirates looked at each other, aghast. Some sat down.

'You all right, Capt'n?' said Franklin.

'Been drinkin' seawater?' said Gregory.

'Never felt better!' growled the Captain.

'Shave? And . . . buy . . . food?' repeated Franklin, feeling his rough beard.

'It's a brilliant idea,' cried Violet, jumping up and down on the platform.

'If it don't work,' said the Pirate Captain, his voice becoming stronger and a little twinkle returning to his eye, 'then I promise you all – we'll go straight back to raidin'!'

The crew looked thoughtful, but not convinced.

'And I'll pay fer everyfink!'

That sealed it.

Chapter 11

The little port of White Rock lay on the south coast of England, nestling between cliffs. It was a quiet little fishing harbour.

One bright and breezy summer's day, when the sea was choppy and white horses crested the waves, a ship sailed straight for the quay. The people on the cliff above the town commented that it was a fine sight to see a ship in full rig skimming the waves at such a speed.

She furled her sails as she approached and slowed into the calm of the harbour, docking neatly with her port side to the harbour wall.

A little crowd came to look at the vessel. And to wonder at its strange occupants.

One by one they disembarked. They were thin and dishevelled but clean-shaven. They wore a bizarre variety of ill-fitting outfits: there was an Admiral, a parson, three gentlemen, a carpenter and a little girl. All had dark and swarthy faces, as if they had been at sea for a long time. Standing on the stone jetty, they wobbled strangely as their sea legs got used to the solid ground.

'Corky!' said the Admiral. 'Me eyes aren't so good – can you read that thar sign?'

'Cr-ea-m teas,' replied a stocky gentleman, blinking through his spectacles.

'Tea? I'm gasping,' said another, taller, gentleman, and began striding down the jetty to the teashop. The others followed. After that the townsfolk followed. This was the most curious band of travellers they had seen in a long while.

The bell tinkled as the odd group entered the teashop. A little lady popped up and smiled uncertainly at them.

'Can I help you?' she asked.

'I'll 'ave tea,' said the Admiral.

'Please,' added the girl, tugging at his elbow. 'You've got to say please here.' The men looked down at her, frowning.

'Cream tea?' asked the lady, counting the group. 'For seven?'

'Twenty-one!' said the biggest gentleman, whose trousers only just covered his knees. 'In – big – mugs.'

'In pots,' called another.

'In big buckets!' shouted the parson.

'*Please*,' added the little girl.

They sat down at a couple of tables and waited. A few boys peered through the window. The girl watched them curiously. One of them stuck out his tongue. The girl stuck hers out back.

Tea came in pots with separate milk. There were mugs and little china plates. They had scones and cream and jam and gallons of tea. They doubled the order to forty-two cream teas and they ate six each. It was absolutely delicious. The Admiral was beaming, the parson humming, the gentlemen scoffing themselves silly. The carpenter, who seemed to be on good terms with all of them, was however, the messiest.

Never had anyone ever made such a mess in the teashop. There were crumbs, blobs of jam and cream, spillages everywhere. Nor had anyone ever eaten so loudly or burped so disgustingly as those men. But the lady didn't mind, for she had never seen her customers enjoy cream teas so much. After all that baking and brewing, she thought it was a pleasure to see some hungry and thirsty men eat and drink with such gusto!

'What have you been doing that you got such powerful appetites?' she asked.

'We been sailing the oceans of the world, ma'am,' said the Admiral, 'from east and west to north and south. Playing cat an' mouse wi' the Portuguese. An' now we is coming home to settle.' Some of the gentlemen seemed surprised at this news.

'Oh. What are you going to settle to then?' asked the lady.

'Ah, well.' The Admiral felt his chin uneasily. He suddenly picked up a spoon and looked at his reflection. 'That depends, it does, on . . . on . . . on . . .'

'The weather,' barked the parson.

'Oh – the weather's very nice here,' said the lady. 'It's the summer season and we've had lots of visitors. Been a good year. Though you wouldn't know it from the people's faces: they're all sad because the circus has gone. Packed up last week it did, after a lovely run. Don't know what to do with themselves now.'

'A circus? What's that then?' asked the carpenter.

'Why, you know – they have tightrope walkers, and gymnasticals and clowns – you should have seen the clowns, tripping over their big feet and banging their noses. How we laughed! There was a flying trapeze too – oooh, daredevil it was – my heart was in my mouth!'

'Shame,' said one of the gentlemen. 'I should ha' liked to see the circus.'

'Well now,' said the Admiral. 'Time to be getting along. An' now, as we usually do, we must p . . . we must p . . . p . . . p . . .' The Admiral blinked. 'We must p . . . p . . . p . . .'

Someone sniggered. Yes, someone definitely sniggered.

'Pay,' said the little girl in a clear voice.

'Quite so,' nodded the Admiral. He pulled out a

large bag and emptied the contents on to the table. Diamonds, rubies, emeralds and gold glittered before them.

'Goodness me,' gasped the lady. 'It won't be that much!'

'Of course not,' grinned the Admiral wickedly. He picked a small gold coin at the edge of the sparkling heap and pushed it towards her. 'Will that do?' he asked.

The lady nodded. The Admiral then put his arm around his treasure and swept it back into his bag.

After tea the pirates took a tour of the town. There were little streets and alleys with whitewashed houses going up the side of the hill. There were taverns and shops and nearby nets hung out to dry. Violet examined everything. She felt the stone houses, she touched the wild flowers growing by the road, she lay on the grass and smelled the earth. In the alleys women and children peeped from doorways. To one side there was a seesaw and a rope swing hanging from a tree. Two little boys were playing there.

'Can I go and play?' asked Violet.

'Course you can,' said the Pirate Captain fondly.

She ran across the grass towards the playground and the pirates watched her go. Freed from the confines of the ship, she ran with her arms outspread.

'Like a bird released from a cage,' said Corky. And watching her, the pirates understood how one day Violet would leave them.

'She needs other children,' said Corky.

'Can't always be a pirate,' whispered Percy.

The others were silent. The Pirate Captain sat down on the grass. He watched her approach the boys, talking to them, circling them.

That night, after they'd stocked up on supplies at the shop, the pirates sat on deck. They'd eaten meat and fresh bread for the first time in months and they felt good. Their bellies were full. They liked this little town. They even liked the feeling of dry land under their feet. Gregory played softly on his accordion. Violet had had a lovely afternoon playing with the other children and now she sat in her favourite place high up in the crow's nest.

'She's thinking of life on land,' said Percy.

'I reckon she'll run away to land!' joked Corky.

Just then little Violet swooped down on her rope swing and tried to snatch the flaming torch that the pirates were sitting next to. 'Get orf!' scolded Gregory. 'You'll hurt yerself.'

There were cheers and whistles from the quay. The pirates hadn't realised some of the townsfolk were sitting there in the darkness watching.

Violet swung back again, past the flaming torch, and landed neatly on the platform. The townsfolk clapped.

In the darkness the Pirate Captain sat bolt upright. 'Lads,' he said in an urgent whisper, 'I 'ave just 'ad an absolute corker of an idea!'

Chapter 12

The Pirate Captain gathered the crew together in a huddle so that the townsfolk could not hear. Then he explained his idea. The pirates groaned.

But Violet jumped up and down, squealing, 'Yes, yes. Oh, please! Let's do it, can we, please?'

The Pirate Captain beamed at her, and looked around at the others. But the pirates were split. Gregory thought it was a good idea, Franklin did not.

'We is pirates, ain't we?' he said. 'Mean and rotten, ain't we?'

Percy agreed. 'I'm a sailor – not a landlubber.'

'But it is worth a try – like we say to Vile – you gotta try.'

'That's right,' said Violet. 'It's a way of making money, not taking money. Come on, don't be pathetic. Let's give it a go. I thought you liked adventure.'

The pirates were put out at this. Of course they liked adventure. Their whole lives were an adventure. They were willing to try anything. What was this little idea, compared to battling with soldiers or facing down a terrible storm at sea?

And anyway, didn't their beloved Violet want it?

They had a vote and the Captain won. The next morning he went to the harbourmaster of the town and booked the place on the jetty for two weeks.

Then he came back and they started work.

First, they took the sails down and began sewing them together. The people watched. Gentlemen sewing? It was very odd. In a little while there was a vast sheet of canvas which grew bigger and bigger as the hours passed and more sails were added. By the end of the morning it was so big that they attached it to the top of the main mast. Then it fanned out like a tent and the ship disappeared from view.

The townsfolk grew more and more curious. What was going on in there? When they asked, the gentlemen just winked at them.

'You'll find out soon enough,' they said.

'What're you doing in there?' the kids in the playground asked Violet. She went there every day when the children got out of school.

'You'll find out,' she said mysteriously.

For five whole days there was a furious sawing and hammering. At the end of a week, a string of fairy lights appeared, sparkling in the darkness over the ship. The next day bunting fluttered from the top of the masts.

The townsfolk became excited. Fairy lights and bunting meant something special. Maybe a party? They watched for balloons. Maybe a wedding? Maybe the opening of a shop or a theatre?

Then a sign went up. It read: 'Saturday 7pm!' That was it. Nothing about *what* was going to happen, only *when* it was going to happen. But they didn't mind – bunting and fairy lights meant something special.

At seven o'clock on Saturday, the Pirate Captain stepped out. He wasn't an Admiral any more – he was a fierce pirate, a mean and rotten pirate – and the people shrank back.

'ARRHARR, me hearties,' he shouted to the

line of people on the quay. 'Line up proper and step this way. Twopence a seat for the thrill o' yer lives. Arrharr!' He had a roll of tickets and immediately began selling them. The people paid their money and streamed in. They were greeted by an amazing sight.

The pirates had constructed a huge tent over the ship. There were benches running in a semi-circle all around the quayside and a ring in the middle on the main deck was covered in sawdust. There were ropes and swings slung from the yardarms; there were coloured flags and lights and above it all a

Jolly Roger and the legend: 'Violet and the Pirate Circus'.

The lights went down. The Pirate Captain stepped into the spotlight. Some people were still chatting.

'Silence,' growled the Captain. He glowered at the audience. Then with a slow screech of scraping metal, he drew out a sword. Silence ran through the crowd like an electric shock, leaving them rigid with attention. 'I'm the Captain and everyone does as I say. That understood?'

The people nodded. They thought they were going to be robbed. The Pirate Captain marched around the ring looking into the eyes of the audience, sitting frozen to their seats. A child whimpered.

'Har, har,' laughed the Captain, realising that the crowd were perhaps a little too frightened of him and might leave before the show. He tried to lighten the mood. 'I'm a pirate,' he told some children at the front and rolled his eyes. 'I is the most frighteningest pirate in the land!' he roared.

Luckily, at that moment a huge barrel of cold water was tipped all over him.

'AAAAHHHH!' he cried, dancing about with the

shock of the cold and shaking himself like a mad dog.

Suddenly, the people started laughing. The dripping Captain spun around and found Corky and Franklin, dressed as pirate clowns, with enormous feet, red noses and giant parrots on their heads, laughing and slapping their knees.

'I'll 'av you, you dirty ducks!' he cried, and marching over, dripping with water, he banged their heads together. The audience laughed more. The Captain turned and grinned. This was better.

'The Circus is open!' he announced as a rubber

brick bounced on his head. 'First Act: Corky the Clown and First mate Frankie.'

Corky was funny and Franklin was stupid. Franklin was fishing in a barrel as Corky tried to move the barrel to do some washing. Every few seconds they tripped up or slipped up and bashed each other. Then Franklin caught a fish, a real fish, from the barrel and they ran off together, Franklin chasing Corky with the fish.

Now the crowd were enjoying themselves.

The next act introduced Violet on the tightrope. Gregory played his accordion, and Percy banged a drum. Violet walked backwards, forwards, jumped up, spun around and pretended to nearly fall. The audience gasped and clapped with relief at the end.

Then Gregory came forward. The Pirate Captain was tied to a board (protesting mightily), and Gregory was blindfolded. He then threw twelve knives at the Captain. Thunk thunk thunk! The knives thudded into the wood, leaving a faint twanging. The Captain looked sick. His hair, hat and trousers were pinned to the board – but no blood was drawn.

Then Big Bron stepped forward. They tied him in chains and ropes. He was the Strongman. They gave him two minutes to break free. With a terrific roar he snapped the bonds in thirty seconds.

The audience cheered and clapped. Then someone pointed to the roof. Violet was there. A tiny figure lit with a lantern high up in the rigging. She swooped down on her swing, across the audience, up to the trapeze at the top of the tent.

Violet jumped from flying trapeze to trapeze, swivelling in the air, somersaulting above the crowd. Sometimes it seemed impossible that she could catch the other trapeze and that she would surely plummet on to the deck.

The audience sighed and gasped. They stood open-mouthed and when it was over, cheered.

At the end of the evening, the crowd clapped and stamped their feet for more.

As the last of the audience filed out, the pirates sat on the deck and drank tea. It was the best start to their new adventure they could wish for.

'We can do that again,' said Corky.

'Better fun than starvin' at sea!' agreed Gregory.

'I says we do this all summer,' said Percy. 'We'll not go hungry, judging from your money bag there.'

''Ow much is there?' asked Franklin.

The Captain turned out the contents. They counted the coins into piles of ten. It was a lot.

'Imagine — every day for a summer. We could live like this,' said Percy.

'What'll happen when everyone's seen us?' asked Franklin.

'We move on round the coast, to the next port. We become a sailing pirate circus.'

'Think how many ports there are in the world we could visit . . .'

'And it's nice for Vile too — she can make friends.'

'An' read more of 'em books.'

'An' go to school.'

'An' be the Pirate on the Trapeze. Wasn't she fantastic?'

'Aye.'

'Where is she?' asked Corky.

They looked up from habit, and saw Violet sitting at the apex of the tent, gazing out at the twinkling lights of the town. She waved to them and the pirates waved back. All at once they understood that Violet was their real treasure, the treasure they'd been looking for all along.